I0721299

Hidden Angels

By

Anabel Baker

Copyright © 2025

ISBN: 978-1-911761-36-5

For my children.

Acknowledgment

This book has been inspired mostly from life events, my beautiful children and my dear sister, who each have always provided me with such immense love and valued support. I am truly honoured for all their encouragement and belief in me to always continue on my life's journey with strength and purpose. They all make me so happy and whole.

To my wonderful and strong mother who has always shown me right from wrong, and showered me with unconditional love.

To my father who was there for me through the important moments and who is now supporting me from the other side.

To Noble Legacy Publishing for all their hard work and support, and for making this possible, I am grateful.

Table of Contents

Chapter 1

Darcy woke up at 4 a.m., after tossing and turning for the past three hours in her old but comfortable bed. She had been experiencing very vivid dreams for several weeks, and was now waking up each night with beads of sweat forming on her forehead and running down each side of her nose. Although the sash window in her bedroom was wide open every night, it did little to deter the heat and subsequent sweating that Darcy endured each time. Even the swirling fan failed to dissipate the rising heat over her body.

For quite some time, Darcy had also been plagued by a constant ringing in her ears, which would intensify at certain times of the day, or sometimes in the presence of others. The ringing, combined with the hum of the relentless fan and the overheating episodes, was beginning to take a toll on her emotional state. It affected her ability to perform at work, and to get through meetings and visits without nodding off or becoming overly anxious.

Darcy was a social worker and enjoyed working with adults of varying ages. Before joining the profession, her sole purpose in life had been to support others to achieve change and to make a difference, however small, in people's lives. Unfortunately, the constraints of the organisation and the lack of resources made this almost impossible for her to achieve. She had recently made the decision to find an alternative path to fulfil her life's goals and help people in whatever way she could, particularly in helping others heal both physically and mentally. A month earlier, she had handed in her notice, determined to embark on a new career path that would offer her purpose and real meaning.

For now, however, Darcy was struggling to get through each night due to her consistent lack of sleep, which left her frustrated and irritable. This, in turn, made it even harder to focus on exploring her new career options and taking the next steps in her life.

As Darcy turned onto her left side for what felt like the thirty-third time that night, she felt something cold and dry crunching beneath her arm. She sat upright and switched on the bedside lamp to find, beside her, a folded piece of white paper with her name scrawled in red ink across the centre.

Darcy was no stranger to unexplainable things. Throughout her life, she had encountered many such experiences. As a young child, her mother often told her she lived in her own little world, and when her name was called, she would completely ignore it, as though she were on another planet. Her mother even took her for a hearing test, but her hearing was perfectly fine. Darcy would also stare into artificial lights for long periods, as if lost in another dimension. She could never recall why this happened or what went on during those moments, and she still couldn't explain it to this day.

During her teenage years, she often experienced visits from souls, or "ghosts" as others might call them, and she could sometimes feel their presence, which terrified her. In her twenties and thirties, these experiences became more intense, as she began to receive messages from departed souls to pass on to the living. Some people accepted these messages gratefully, while others did not, depending on their beliefs. The only issue was that Darcy usually received such communications while under the influence of alcohol.

A psychic medium had once warned her never to "mix spirits with spirits", and after taking this advice to heart, Darcy made great efforts to protect herself. In time, the communications ceased, much to her relief, as some of the messages had previously landed her in difficult situations.

On one occasion, a little girl's spirit visited her. The girl had been murdered, but her body was never found. She begged Darcy to help find her killer and her remains. The encounter placed Darcy in a delicate situation, as it had occurred while she was out drinking with friends. It was impossible to pursue it later, as she never received messages when sober, and she couldn't remain intoxicated for the rest of her life.

Eventually, Darcy stopped drinking and withdrew from social events. She chose instead to follow a different path, embracing spirituality and healing. She soon discovered how much personal healing she needed and how much buried trauma she had to confront and release before she could live freely and peacefully.

Now, as Darcy stared at the note that had been attached to her sweaty arm, she gazed at it for several minutes, her mind swirling with emotions and possible explanations. Then, in a sudden moment of shock, she realised she recognised the handwriting. It was from someone who could not possibly have written to her.

Chapter 2

Darcy carefully unfolded the piece of paper, aware not to tear it since it was now slightly damp in places from her perspiration. At that precise moment, a strong gust of wind blew through the open window and around her body. The cold air brought a moment of comfort to Darcy, lowering her temperature by at least one degree. Yet, at the same time, it terrified her, senses on high alert, and goosebumps covered her entire body.

Darcy knew this note was written by her beautiful, kind, and mischievous sister, but that seemed impossible, as her sister had gone missing twenty-two years ago, along with her other sister. Both her sisters were younger than her, one by four years and the other by two. They had always been very close and spent much of their time together, laughing and growing side by side.

Her sisters, Penelope and Faith, were out together at an event in the local hotel at the time of their disappearance. Darcy was unable to join them due to a prior engagement. However, they maintained contact throughout the evening via text message. The messages described how boring the event was and how Darcy wasn't missing much. Their last message mentioned that they had met some nice gentlemen who were treating them to very nice cocktails. Darcy enjoyed their conversations, finding them rather hilarious, and she was happy that they were beginning to enjoy their evening.

When neither of her sisters replied to her last message, sent at 11 p.m., she became very concerned. Her sisters always responded to her messages—even if it was the following day. When Darcy still received no response by the following afternoon, she drove to both of their homes, searching each one from top to bottom. It was clear neither of the beds had been slept in, and there was no sign of either of them. Darcy was on high alert; her heart raced so fast that she could hear the echoes in her ears. Panic enveloped her entire being, causing heart palpitations and full-body shakes.

Darcy knew in her gut and felt in her bones that something sinister had occurred that night. She immediately contacted the police, providing all the details and informing them that both her sisters' phones had been switched off after numerous attempts to reach them. Unfortunately, there were no tracking devices available then as there are today. Despite the police investigation, Darcy's own efforts, media appeals, and missing posters, there was nothing—zilch, nada. No information or leads about what had happened to her beautiful sisters.

Police speculated that they might have run off together, but Darcy questioned, "Why?" There was no reason they would. They were both happy in their lives and homes—carefree and full of joy. It made no sense that they would have disappeared voluntarily, especially after a hotel event. The most obvious conclusion was that they had been abducted, either from the event or shortly after leaving the hotel.

There had been no CCTV coverage back then as there is now. No link was ever found between her sisters and anyone who might have wished them harm. Both were loved deeply by everyone in their lives, including Darcy. The case was never solved, but Darcy never gave up searching—it consumed her entirely. Although she always had a nagging feeling that her sisters were still alive, she never found the breakthrough she so desperately needed.

Darcy endured the trauma mostly alone. Some

friends tried to help in the beginning, but eventually, they all drifted away. Her parents had passed away four years before her sisters' disappearance, leaving her to fight through the pain on her own. In some ways, she was grateful that her parents had not lived to endure the heartbreak of losing Penelope and Faith; she doubted they would have survived it.

Darcy still remembers the pain and anguish she felt at that time. She remains certain that her sisters were taken— she instinctively knows this is the only possible explanation. The "who" and the "why" still consume her to this day. Though the police called it speculation, Darcy has always believed her sisters were abducted by strangers for the purposes of human and sex trafficking. Deep down, she knows it. The only question that remains is—are her sisters still alive?

Darcy sat on the edge of the bed, her hands shaking uncontrollably, her mouth dry like sawdust, and her eyes blinking rapidly, forcing tears to roll down her cheeks. She hesitantly peeled back the first layer of the folded paper, nervous to see what was written inside—and how this note had appeared on her bed in the middle of the night.

The note read:

Look for us, we are waiting. We love you. Latitude: 55.5424369 / Longitude: -444.2169336.

The note was finished off with a green heart and a yellow balloon.

Chapter 3

Darcy could not move. She was frozen on the edge of her bed, still holding the note in her trembling hands, finding it difficult to breathe. She was in complete shock. Gut-wrenching spasms coursed through her as she knew, deep within her body and soul, that her beloved sisters were still alive. More than that, she was certain the note was from them—their shared signs, a green heart and a yellow balloon, were unmistakable.

Years ago, Darcy and her sisters had agreed upon these angelic symbols during a conversation about divine guidance. Whenever they sought answers from their spirit guides, these signs would appear—sometimes in books, on social media, on clothing, or even out in nature—just when they were needed most. Penelope had chosen the green heart and yellow balloon as her signs, and no one else apart from Darcy and Faith knew their meaning.

Yet, Darcy could not fathom how a handwritten note had ended up in her bed without anyone physically placing it there. Did Penelope—or someone acting on her behalf— enter her home to leave it? The thought confused her deeply.

Acting on instinct, she jumped from the bed and quickly dressed in a T-shirt and shorts, beads of sweat forming across her body. Her mind raced, sifting through countless thoughts as she tried to decide her next move. She knew she couldn't go to the police; they would likely assume she had finally suffered a breakdown.

There was only one option—to follow her sister's instructions and embark on this journey of discovery alone. The note contained a sequence of numbers, clearly coordinates, which she entered into her maps app. She waited anxiously as the image loaded, her heart pounding so fast she thought she might faint. She focused on her breathing: three deep inhalations through the nose, hold for three, then exhale through the mouth for three. She repeated the process nine times until her body stopped shaking and her mind grew clearer.

When Darcy finally glanced at her screen, she saw a vast stretch of land in the middle of nowhere—a tiny pinprick in the centre of an immense forest, with rivers running alongside. How could her sisters possibly be there? Unless they were hiding on some remote farmland, it seemed impossible. No buildings were visible.

Finding this strange, Darcy closed her eyes and tried to connect with her quiet inner space—to reach her divine spirit team. She had always wondered why they had never revealed her sisters' whereabouts, but she knew from experience that deeply personal matters were rarely shared. To her, this was simply a law of the universe.

Sitting in silence, she asked her question and waited. No voice, no vision. She asked again, pleading for guidance—but still, nothing. Then, a warm, tingling sensation spread through her body. She recognised it immediately. It was confirmation from the universe—her sign to trust her heart and follow the message her sisters had sent.

Darcy quickly grabbed her rucksack and filled it with everything she thought she might need for the long journey ahead, as the map indicated the location was 366 miles from her home. She pondered how her sisters could have been so close all this time, yet still so far away. She packed snacks, water, clothing, and, most importantly, her personal alarm and taser. Darcy had bought the taser from an unknown website, knowing she needed to protect herself and stay prepared for any unexpected danger, especially in a world that felt increasingly chaotic, and after her sisters' mysterious abduction.

Once packed, Darcy rushed into her spacious lounge, where everything sat in its rightful place. She was always meticulously neat, and if anything appeared even slightly out of alignment, she noticed instantly. To her, such signs often meant her spirit guides were present—sometimes offering comfort, sometimes issuing a warning. Scanning the pristine room, she searched for anything that might be out of place. Then, out of the corner of her eye, she noticed something blinking. Turning slowly, she saw sunlight streaming through a narrow gap in the curtains, reflecting off her silver angel ornament—one that Penelope had crafted for her during a pottery class.

Darcy stepped closer and realised the ornament had been moved, tilted about six degrees to the right. In that instant, she knew it was confirmation. Her sisters were guiding her, leading her towards the truth she had sought for more than twenty years. A wave of relief washed over her as she felt her divine team surrounding her, ready to walk beside her on this journey of discovery.

Moving swiftly through the house, Darcy thanked her team of light and hurried outside to her car. The morning sunlight gleamed through the trees lining the street, beyond which stretched a mesmerising field of sunflowers. They seemed to dance and smile in the golden light, nodding their heads as though encouraging her to go.

A sharp jolt pierced her heart, and she whispered to herself, "This is it. This is what you've hoped for all these years. Go and bring your sisters home."

With that, she grasped the car door handle, feeling a surge of energy rush through her arm, filling her with strength and purpose. As she settled into the cold leather seat, a chill ran down her spine—part nerves, part anticipation. What would she find alone in that forest? Something wonderful—or something harrowing? Darcy quickly dismissed the darker thought. Determined, she entered the coordinates into her satnav and set off, following the blinking light on the screen as it guided her towards the unknown.

Chapter 4

An hour into the drive, running almost on autopilot, Darcy pressed the button to lower her window, craving a rush of fresh air. She felt as though she couldn't get enough of it—the panic and uncertainty of what awaited her were making her heart race uncontrollably. Her thoughts spiralled in every direction. What if this is all a trap? What if I find my sisters, but they're not really them anymore? What if they're gone, and my heart finally breaks for good?

What if, what if, what if. That was all she could think.

Determined not to drown in fear, Darcy tried to flip the script. She repeated to herself, My sisters are safe. They're healthy. I will find them in the exact place I'm heading to. The affirmation steadied her—though only for five minutes—before panic crept back in. To calm her nerves, she decided to stop at the nearest petrol station, which appeared on her satnav barely a mile ahead.

Outside, the weather began to shift. The first drops of rain tapped against the windscreen, quickly multiplying. She let them fall, filling the glass, her mind darkening once more. If this is all a ruse—if I don't find them—my life will shatter again. She couldn't imagine continuing the lonely existence she'd tried, and failed, to build. She just felt so lost.

She longed for the warmth and love of her sisters—for their laughter, their energy, the unconditional affection that had once surrounded her. Her so-called friends had long since drifted away, leaving her with nothing but memories of what she'd lost. What was the point of it all without love? she thought bitterly. And if I do find them—what love will they have left to give? What horrors might they have endured? Will they be so broken they can't love again?

A flash of movement on the windscreen snapped her back. She flicked on the wipers just in time to see the petrol station emerge about a hundred metres ahead. She wiped at the wetness on her cheek, only then realising she'd been crying.

Darcy pulled into the forecourt beside the pump but hesitated. She didn't want to face the dreary world outside—or the possibility of having to speak to strangers. Her thoughts were spiralling again, the edges of darkness closing in.

A sudden noise outside startled her. Snapping out of

her trance, she stepped from the car and began refuelling on instinct, her movements mechanical. Once the tank was full, she trudged towards the store, silently hoping no one would meet her gaze.

The wind had grown stronger, the rain now lashing against the cars and windows. Darcy pulled her coat tighter around her, bracing against the chill, and pushed through the door into the warmth of the shop. Bedraggled and weary, she handed her money to the attendant, forcing a weak smile.

The man behind the till offered a few cheerful words, trying to lighten the gloomy day, but Darcy couldn't bring herself to respond. She gave a faint nod instead and hurried back outside, eager to retreat from both the rain and the world.

Darcy managed to get back into the car unscathed and drove away with renewed determination. All would be well—she would find her sisters and bring them home safely.

For the next two hours, she drove in silence, accompanied only by the hum of the engine and the cool breeze drifting through the half-open window. The rain had cleared at last, revealing golden rays of sunlight breaking through perfectly formed clouds. She drove on autopilot, following the endless straight roads that stretched ahead, the red dot on the satnav drawing ever closer.

Fields blurred past on either side—vivid poppies, wildflowers, grazing sheep and cows, and stretches of farmland where crops were being ploughed. Excitement and anxiety mingled within her, bubbling up in her stomach as the destination mark crept nearer on the glowing screen.

The satnav's voice suddenly broke the stillness: "In one hundred yards, turn right." The unexpected sound made Darcy jump; it had been quiet for so long. She steered off the main road, tyres crunching over gravel as the car jolted from side to side along a narrow lane. Following it down, she spotted a small lay-by to the left just as the voice instructed her to "take a sharp left turn."

Darcy braked sharply and peered around. "There is no left turn!" she called out in frustration. Ahead, a long metal fence stretched between two thick hedgerows. Surely I'm not meant to go through there? she thought, glancing back at the satnav. The red dot marking her destination sat firmly in the middle of the adjoining field.

Before her lay a sprawling poppy field, framed by

mountains and trees in every direction. The sight was breathtaking. For a long moment, she stayed in the car, transfixed by the beauty before her, confusion washing over her in waves. Why would my sisters be in the middle of a poppy field? she wondered. What could this possibly mean?

Gathering her courage, Darcy climbed out of the car, stiff and awkward from the long drive down the bumpy country road. She made her way to the metal gate and was relieved to find it unlatched. Pushing it open, she winced as it squeaked loudly before swinging wide.

Returning to the car, she drove slowly into the field, following the red dot that blinked on her screen. Moments later, the satnav announced: "You have reached your destination."

Darcy switched off the engine and stared ahead. The silence was heavy. No buildings. No movement. No sign of life. Just the endless sea of poppies swaying in the gentle breeze. Then her eyes caught something—a long rectangular mound of freshly heaped earth, just off to the right.

Her breath caught in her throat. It looked, unmistakably, like a grave.

Chapter 5

Darcy froze in her seat. Her heart pounded wildly, each beat echoing in her ears. Her breathing turned rapid and shallow, and her entire body began to shake. She didn't want to move—didn't want to get out of that car. She stared at the mound of earth before her for what felt like a lifetime, her thoughts spiralling into chaos. Why would her sisters lead her here? Had something unimaginable happened after she received the note? Was there something she still couldn't comprehend?

At last, Darcy forced herself to act. She opened the car door with trembling hands and stepped out, summoning every ounce of courage she had left. Her legs quivered beneath her as she tried to steady her breath, counting slowly to calm her racing pulse.

She moved towards the mound, hesitant and wary. Then, out of nowhere, a white butterfly drifted past her face, brushing so close she could feel the air from its wings. It landed gently atop the earthen heap—on the rubble of what looked unmistakably like a grave.

Darcy sank to her knees beside a cluster of poppies, her heart breaking all over again. She called out to her spirit team—begged them—to speak to her, to soothe her, to bring her comfort and clarity. Closing her eyes, she tried to empty her mind of the endless questions and confusion. She sat in stillness, breathing deliberately, waiting for a sign… a single word… anything.

A cool breeze swept across her clammy skin. The sun, now breaking through the clouds, warmed her tear-streaked face. On any other day, she might have welcomed the feeling, but now it offered no comfort, no peace.

Then, after several long minutes of silence, she heard it—five simple words, soft yet unmistakable: "Dig and you will find her."

Darcy's stomach twisted. Find who? she wondered in horror. She has two sisters—wasn't she meant to find them alive? For a moment, she thought of running back to the car and driving away, escaping whatever truth awaited beneath the soil. But something within her refused to leave.

With trembling hands, Darcy began to dig. She clawed at the earth with frantic urgency, dirt collecting beneath her fingernails, coating her hands in mud. She dug until her fingers ached and her palms burned, until her breath came in short gasps. Then, suddenly, she felt something solid—hard, yet yielding beneath her touch. Metal, perhaps.

She tore away another layer of soil, her hands raw and brown with dirt, until the shape beneath was fully exposed.

And then she saw her.

Among the loose earth and Darcy's own tears, lay Penelope—her beautiful, kind, quirky sister. She was stretched out, arms folded across her chest, as though she had gently placed them there herself.

Darcy's breath caught. She didn't know how long it took for a body to decompose, but Penelope didn't look as though she had been gone for long. Her face was serene, her skin pale but intact. She looked as if she had simply drifted into sleep and had not yet awakened.

Darcy shakily placed her hand on top of Penelope's right hand—it was ice cold. She could not believe what she was seeing. None of it made sense. Shock and despair consumed her, and she began to scream until her lungs emptied. Her cries echoed across the surrounding hills, reverberating through the poppy field where she now knelt beside her sister.

She crawled closer, gathering Penelope in her arms, pressing trembling lips to her forehead, speaking softly as if trying to wake her from a long sleep. "Come on now," she whispered through tears. "It's time to wake up and open those sparkling eyes of yours. I've waited so long to talk to you, to touch you, to laugh with you, to love you. Please, Penelope... please wake up now."

Darcy stayed there, holding her sister for what felt like an eternity—perhaps an hour or more—until the distant hum of a tractor broke the silence. Carefully, she laid Penelope back down, arranging her arms just as she'd found them. With shaking hands, she began to cover her sister again, returning the earth she had so desperately clawed away. No one must find her, not yet. Darcy needed time to think.

Numb, she staggered back to the car, climbed inside, and sped away in the opposite direction. She drove aimlessly, barely aware of the world around her, until she reached a small village nestled among the hills. Flowers bloomed from every corner, brightening the cobbled street that led to a large yellow-bricked building with a golden sign reading The Bolthole.

Next to the restaurant was a wide car park, beyond which she caught sight of a lake glimmering under the sunlight. Darcy pulled into an empty space, relieved to find only one other car parked nearby. Solitude was all she wanted now.

She stepped out, following a narrow path through the bushes that opened onto the lake. Swans and ducks drifted peacefully across the surface, their lives untouched by the chaos that had shattered hers. Darcy wished she could swap places with them—simple, undisturbed, unbroken. But today was, without question, the worst day of her life.

She sank onto one of four wooden benches carved beautifully beneath the willow and sycamore trees. Time blurred. For two long hours, she sat motionless, debating whether to contact the detective who had handled her sisters' disappearance years ago—or to stay silent and uncover the truth herself.

At last, she made her choice. She would tell no one—not yet. She would keep Penelope's death to herself and follow the instructions her sister had left behind in the makeshift grave.

There was still one sister left to find.

Chapter 6

Darcy sat in the car, staring numbly into the distance, watching swallows dive and swirl against the deep blue sky. She curled her body into a tight ball and remained in the foetal position for what felt like hours. Her heart ached as she sobbed uncontrollably, grieving for her sister—lost once over twenty years ago, and again today.

Yet, amid her devastation, there was a sliver of comfort in having seen Penelope one final time. Her beautiful face, her dark curls, her flawless skin—she looked almost untouched by time. Darcy marvelled at how little she seemed to have aged and wondered what Penelope had endured all these years without her by her side. Judging by the state of her body, she couldn't have been in the ground for more than a day or two; there was no sign of decay. Darcy silently promised she would return for Penelope once she found Faith—praying, pleading, that her second sister was still alive.

Eventually, she forced herself to sit upright, her limbs stiff and heavy. She drew in a long breath and focused her mind on the set of markings she had noticed earlier—

etched faintly along the inside of Penelope's right arm. When she had held her sister close, she had seen them clearly and instinctively taken a photograph on her phone. The markings, written in what appeared to be red ink, read:

"I am sorry, I love you. Find Faith across the border at this location-Lat: 10.57235, Long: 114.824.

Please hurry. Talk soon xxx"

At the end of the message was a tiny blue butterfly—Faith's symbol.

Darcy studied the photo closely. The handwriting was unmistakably Penelope's. Only she and her sisters knew about the blue butterfly. But Darcy still couldn't comprehend how Penelope had managed to write the note that appeared in her bed—or how she had etched this message onto her own arm before dying, without anyone noticing.

She had always been open to the unknown, accustomed to the strange workings of the spirit world, but never had she witnessed anything like this. Still, she knew Penelope had always been a determined soul—strong, brave, and deeply connected to forces unseen. If anyone could bridge the gap between life and death to leave such signs, it was her. Perhaps, in time, her divine team of light would reveal the how and the when.

Gathering herself once more, Darcy entered the new coordinates into the satnav and waited for it to load. When the route appeared, she gasped—the journey would take eleven hours, including a ferry crossing.

She glanced at her rucksack, mentally checking its contents. She might need to buy a few extra items along the way—perhaps a change of clothes for a disguise. It was best if no one recognised her or discovered her purpose. She'd also need to refuel before setting off again.

But right now, one thing took priority. She needed the toilet. With a weary sigh, she grabbed her bag and stepped out of the car, heading towards the restaurant.

Chapter 7

On her way to the shops, Darcy remained puzzled over how the messages had reached her when her sister had clearly already passed over. She told herself it must be the workings of the divine. Darcy's own belief was that a soul's passing is already orchestrated and planned before entering life on earth. When a soul's purpose is fulfilled, its time here ends and it returns home. Unless, of course, it is not yet the right time for a soul to pass—then, divine intervention occurs to prevent its departure, allowing it more time to experience and learn.

Darcy was certain that this was Penelope's time to return home. However painful it was, she found solace in knowing her sister was now in a place of love and light, free from pain and trauma. She trusted that Penelope would communicate again when the time was right. For now, Darcy relied on her divine team for protection and guidance as she continued this harrowing journey to find Faith.

An hour later, after driving through residential streets and along dual carriageways, Darcy arrived at a small stretch of village shops. The scene was picturesque—bright flowers in full bloom adorned the storefronts, and the buildings, made from old cream-coloured stone, carried the charm of another era. The entire street felt timeless, as if she had stepped back in history. A warm tingle ran down her spine.

She parked in one of the empty spaces outside a shop with a beautifully painted sign scattered with butterflies, surrounding the words "Blue Orchid." Looking around, she saw the usual mix of village shops—a patisserie, a hardware store, a coffee shop, a high-end clothing boutique, and a small convenience store. But it was Blue Orchid that drew her in. From the window display of trinkets and clothing, she could tell it was a gift shop—and more importantly, the name spoke to her. The blue orchid had been Faith's favourite flower. Darcy instinctively knew this shop would have exactly what she needed, and perhaps, offer some comfort or guidance too.

As she stepped out of the car, a large brown-and-white feather drifted past her, hovering for a few seconds before being carried away on the gentle breeze. Taking it as another sign, she entered the shop and was immediately enveloped by a wave of heavenly scents—cinnamon, vanilla, watermelon, green fig, and honeysuckle. The air was thick with warmth and sweetness, wrapping around her like an embrace.

The store was filled with treasures—candles, jewellery, sweets, and clothes of every kind. Under different circumstances, Darcy could have spent hours there, captivated by the sensory harmony of fragrances and colours. But today, her purpose was clear—she needed to get in and out as quickly as possible.

She moved briskly through the aisles, picking up a baseball cap, sunglasses, and a light summer scarf—enough to disguise her face if needed. Within eleven minutes, she had what she came for and joined the queue. The shop's atmosphere was welcoming, the energy calm and soothing. The staff and customers alike were cheerful and friendly, the cashier even attempting small talk. For a brief moment, Darcy almost felt at peace.

Although Darcy would have loved to make small talk with the other shoppers, she simply didn't have the time. Instead, she offered a polite smile, murmured a few words, and hurried on her way.

Once back in the car, she couldn't shake the feeling of familiarity she'd had with the cashier—as though she had known her for years. Dismissing the thought, Darcy reached into the shopping bag and began taking out the items one by one. That was when she noticed the receipt. Four words were written across the bottom, presumably by the cashier: "Have a safe journey, D."

Her mind reeled. She looked up towards the shopfront and, through the window, saw the cashier standing on the other side of the glass, smiling and waving directly at her. The gesture sent a shiver down Darcy's spine but also filled her with reassurance. To her, it was confirmation that she was being protected and guided—that she was still on the right path.

Darcy smiled faintly, raised her hand in return, and gave a small nod before slipping on her disguise. She placed the cap on her head, pulled the sunglasses over her eyes, and wound the scarf around her neck, tugging it up over her chin. Opening her rucksack, she checked that everything was still there. Her taser rested on top.

Feeling a flicker of safety and renewed focus, she started the engine and drove away from the unforgettable

little street, confident she had everything she might need—
just in case.

33

Her next stop was the petrol station, before the long
hour's drive to the port.

Chapter 8

Darcy stopped off for fuel, proceeding through the motions on autopilot once again, but intentionally keeping herself out of sight of the forecourt cameras. After a short drive through the countryside, she boarded the ferry, watching as the sun slowly drifted down into the abyss. It was a striking sunset that held her transfixed in her seat for at least half an hour, wishing she could have shared that view with her sisters over the past twenty years. She hadn't given up all hope, though, as she could still intuitively sense that Faith was alive, for how much longer, she didn't know.

Darcy's eyelids grew heavy, and she almost drifted off while watching the fading sun, realising she hadn't slept for twenty hours. Reaching over to the back seat, she pulled out a fluffy blanket, reclined the seat with the lever, and quickly fell into a deep sleep. With many hours on the ferry ahead, she made the most of the night to rest before facing whatever awaited her on the other side.

She woke several times to the rhythmic flow of the water beneath her and the various sounds surrounding her, footsteps passing by and the clanking of the boat. Despite her exhaustion and grief, sleep remained elusive. Eventually, she decided to go up on deck to find something to eat and drink.

The clock on the dashboard read 3:33 a.m., and Darcy figured it was as good a time as any to have something to build her strength. She tried to avoid unhealthy food and opted for eggs and cheese. Although doubtful the ferry's food would meet her usual standards, she knew anything would do at this point. To her surprise, there were plenty of fruits and yoghurts on offer, along with hot food such as a full English breakfast. She chose scrambled eggs with tomatoes on sourdough toast, surprisingly tasty and satisfying. Sitting outside with her coffee, she warmed her hands against the chill of the night air and the sea spray that rose against the sides of the boat in the gusty winds.

She was becoming increasingly anxious as time passed, bringing her closer to the moment she would have to leave the boat and its safety. She had no idea what awaited her in the final part of her journey. Darcy tried to conjure up images of what her sister might look like now and couldn't escape the harrowing thoughts of what she may have endured over all these years.

Darcy had always imagined that both her sisters had run off to live a magical life somewhere far away, fulfilling their dreams, a comforting illusion that allowed her to keep breathing and living without them. She refused to dwell on the unimaginable reality of what their lives might have become, or the abuse and pain they may have suffered, as doing so would have broken her completely, destroying any hope and stopping her from continuing the search, perhaps even driving her to join Penelope in her fate. Darcy knew she had to stay strong for Faith. As long as she kept receiving these messages and felt guided, nothing would stop her, even if it meant putting herself in danger.

Darcy knew how to change her appearance quickly and how to adopt different personas when necessary. For this next stage of her journey, she hoped she could deliver the best performance of her life. She could feel the presence of her divine team, though they were quiet now, a sign, she sensed, that she must face this part of the path alone, without interference or influence from beyond.

She realised she had been sitting in the blustery cold wind for quite some time, and when she checked her watch, it confirmed she had been shivering on deck for a couple of hours. Pulling her scarf higher over her cold, wet face, she tightened her coat around her body and made her way back to the car, struggling to walk in a straight line due to the motion of the boat. Once inside, she wrapped herself in the blanket again to warm up.

Another twenty-two minutes and the vehicles would begin offloading once the boat docked. Darcy started the engine, turned the heaters on full blast to defrost completely, and switched the satnav back on. Just over a two-hour drive, and she would finally see her sister.

The ferry docked at the harbour, and everyone stirred from their slumber, hurrying to their vehicles. Darcy drove off the ferry, showed her passport to border control, and crossed the vast bridge that spanned the river separating the town beyond.

"Not long now, Faith. Not long," she whispered.

Chapter 9

Darcy took in the passing sights and landscapes in brief moments between concentrating on the unfamiliar route ahead. It was a gloomy day, perfectly matching her mood. Her mind was consumed by a mixture of thoughts, one persistent question echoing louder than the rest: What if she's going to lose Faith in the same awful way she lost Penelope? Or what if she never finds her at all?

Darcy pushed the dark thoughts aside and forced herself to focus on the positive. I will find Faith, and she is alive, she repeated silently. She switched on the radio in search of some light music, but it did little to comfort her. Instead, it seemed to make her even more aware of the heaviness of her situation. With a sigh, she turned it off and decided to stop at the next service station for a toilet break and a hot drink. She desperately needed caffeine, and a moment to gather her thoughts away from the confines of the car.

After an hour of solid driving, Darcy found a pleasant café within a service area. The warm scent of freshly baked croissants and strong coffee filled the air. She chose a table tucked away at the back of the room, far from prying eyes and the bustle of other travellers. Her cap, glasses, and scarf remained firmly in place; she had no desire to draw attention to herself as she waited for the server to approach.

Within five minutes, a woman appeared at her table. Her name badge read Marilyn. She had a genuine smile and short, bouncing blonde curls, appearing to be somewhere in her forties, though Darcy was never particularly good at guessing people's ages. Feeling the loneliness of her long journey, and realising she hadn't spoken properly to anyone for a week, just a few polite exchanges here and there, Darcy decided to make conversation.

Returning Marilyn's warm smile, she asked, "Do you know this area very well?"

"Oh yes," Marilyn replied cheerfully. "I've lived around here most of my life. I've only travelled abroad a handful of times, a shame, really. I always dreamed of seeing the world when I was younger, having all sorts of adventures. But no, I'm still here, and I suppose I'll stay here for the rest of my days. Still, I'm settled and content enough." She paused, then asked, "Where are you travelling from?"

Darcy hesitated before answering. She didn't want to reveal too much, wary of any possible complications later on. After a brief moment, she said, "Oh, I live about six hours away. I'm meeting someone to discuss a business opportunity."

She showed Marilyn the note she had scribbled down from her satnav and asked, "Would you happen to know anything about this place? I believe it's about an hour or so from here."

Marilyn looked at the name of the area and the exact location Darcy was heading towards. As she read, Darcy noticed a sudden change in her expression, the colour drained from Marilyn's face, replaced by a look of pure horror.

Marilyn tried to speak, but no sound came from her mouth; her eyes looked wide and panicked. Darcy waited for several minutes until Marilyn composed herself and whispered, "Why on earth would anyone ask you to meet them there, of all places? That place is known for keeping people locked up against their will. It's supposedly a psychiatric hospital, but most locals say otherwise. Rumours have circulated for years that it's actually a front for human and sex trafficking, and the conditions inside are unimaginable. Nobody can get in. The local police have received numerous complaints and requests to search the place, but as far as I know, they've never followed up on the locals' concerns, they're no doubt being paid off by whoever runs the operation. I believe people have taken photographs of the comings and goings and logged times and dates, but nothing has been investigated. Who are you meeting there? It seems very suspicious. I really hope you don't go after everything I've just told you."

Darcy could not breathe; she began to hyperventilate. Marilyn recognised it immediately and tried to calm her, guiding Darcy through deep-breathing techniques and asking her to keep her eyes fixed on Marilyn's. She held Darcy's hands and talked her through each step. Gradually Darcy's breathing slowed and became more even. Another server, having seen Darcy's distress from about ten metres away, automatically brought her a glass of water, which she accepted gratefully. She turned back to Marilyn's worried face.

"I'm very sorry about that," Darcy said. "Thank you so much for helping me. I'm not actually meeting anyone there, I'm searching for my sister, who's been missing for over twenty years. This is the location where I'm supposed to find her. Please don't ask how I know; I just do."

Marilyn shook her head in disbelief and looked wary of Darcy's admission. She knelt in front of Darcy, took her hands again, and said, "Well, if this is where you're going to find your sister after all these years, then I'm coming with you. I will not let you go into a place like that alone; neither of us knows what we'll be walking into. Be prepared: this could either blow the whole operation wide open and help save a lot of people, or we could be the ones who end up joining those poor souls there, with no escape for us either. I do know a few good people who could help with weapons if needed, planning a mission, and finding entry points. Actually, this place has been on our radar for some time, but we've never had solid evidence to back up the rumours. Now we can go full steam ahead with this mission."

Darcy stared numbly at Marilyn, unable to believe that this woman kneeling before her could show such kindness, warmth, and determination to help a complete stranger. She was amazed. Struggling to find her voice, Darcy choked out the words, "You really can't do that for me. It's too dangerous, you'll be putting yourself in harm's way. I can't let you do that; you don't even know me."

Marilyn shook her head firmly. "Look, it's about time someone did something to help those people and bring the ones responsible to justice. If the police won't act, then we will. It's not in my nature to ignore this or to turn my back on you, or on anyone suffering like that. I won't stand by and let this continue, and I certainly won't let you go through it alone. Let's do this."

With that, Marilyn pulled Darcy up from the chair, slung Darcy's rucksack over her own shoulder, and called out to her colleague, "I have to go, it's an emergency! See you tomorrow!"

Darcy and Marilyn ran out of the café and into Darcy's car, breathless, adrenaline surging through their bodies. Marilyn pulled her mobile from her bag, dialled the tenth number on her call list, spoke briefly to the person on the other end, and hung up.

"All good to go," she said confidently. "We'll drive

to this location and pick up my friends on the way."

Marilyn read out the directions at each turn and junction. As Darcy gripped the steering wheel, she felt a tingling sensation flow up and down her arms and through her hands, a reassuring sign that she was meant to meet Marilyn and that she was still on the right path.

Chapter 10

As Darcy drove through the quiet residential streets, a yellow balloon drifted past, floating low along the side of the car. She looked around to see if a child might have let it go, but there wasn't a single person in sight. A sudden realisation struck her, this was another sign from Penelope, a confirmation to press on full steam ahead. She longed to hear her sister's voice, to draw strength and hope from her words, but even so, she felt deeply grateful for the signs she had been receiving along her journey, gentle nudges urging her to keep going.

The streets they passed were neat and orderly, with well-kept shrubs and blossom trees lining the pavements, yet to Darcy it all felt strangely unreal, as though she were moving through an illusion. The surroundings seemed eerie, and there was no sound, not a voice, not even the distant hum of another car. She expected to see someone stepping out of a house, or at least another vehicle on the road, but there was nothing. Only silence. Darcy didn't quite understand what it meant, but she knew she didn't like the feeling. Perhaps her senses were preparing her for what was to come.

The uneasy stillness grew heavier inside and outside the car. To distract herself, Darcy turned her attention to Marilyn, who sat beside her with her hands trembling slightly in her lap.

"Are you all right, Marilyn?" Darcy asked softly. "You seem on edge, which is completely understandable, may I add, but it's making me even more nervous. Who exactly are these people we're meeting?"

Marilyn turned her pale, anxious face towards Darcy and replied in a shaky voice, "I'm just nervous about what we're walking into. I've heard the terrible stories about that place, and I can't help but imagine the worst. I do want to help you, and all those people who might be trapped there, but it's frightening to think we could be walking straight into the hands of those monsters ourselves. Still," she added, taking a deep breath, "I've got friends and acquaintances who are going to help us. They'll be with us every step of the way, so we shouldn't worry too much. They're good people, a bit rough around the edges, perhaps, but good all the same. They have to be, to get things done and bring justice to the ones who need it most."

Darcy took a deep breath and questioned herself

silently. Is this really the right path for me? Would it be fair to put these honourable people in danger just to save my sister? She longed to hear more, and with a small nod, encouraged Marilyn to continue.

Marilyn's voice grew steadier as she spoke. "They're what some people might call a vigilante group. They put themselves in extremely dangerous situations, working entirely without police backing, because they're determined to keep this country and its people, safe. They understand how long the legal process can take and how much evidence is required before any action is taken, so they handle things themselves.

"They carry out reconnaissance first and gather as much background information as possible before attempting any mission. They're professionals, they don't take anything on unless it's been fully vetted by the team. And don't worry," she added quickly, "they never intentionally harm anyone to reach those who need rescuing, but they do use self-defence techniques when necessary.

"Most of the group are ex-military, and their purpose is to fight for a better world. To achieve that, they must confront and eliminate the evil that threatens it, to protect the innocent and create safety and compassion for both our generation and the next.

"I've been part of this group for years now and have taken part in many missions with them. It's gut-wrenching and incredibly difficult to witness what we see, but our determination to bring justice and peace keeps us going. It may take another decade, or even longer, but the most important role any of us can have in life is to help achieve safety and peace for all, because that's what every person deserves.

"Yes, we risk injury, even death, but we all agree that this purpose, this mission, is a sacrifice for the greater good. What's the point of living if not with love, happiness, and unity?

"If you feel you'd rather go alone to find your sister, that's entirely your choice. You have no obligation to join forces with my team. Do what feels right to you. Just know that if you choose to accept our help, we'll be with you one hundred per cent every step of the way."

Darcy considered Marilyn's words and concluded that the only thing stopping her from agreeing to team up was the thought of putting these people in harm's way because of her quest. She understood the risks of doing the mission alone and was prepared to face them, but she also recognised the obstacles and dangers that might cost her life and Faith's. In the end, there was only one option that gave her the best chance of keeping them both safe: allow Marilyn and her group to accompany her on this unpredictable, terrifying rescue.

Turning to Marilyn, gratitude thick in her voice, she said, "Okay, I agree. Get your group involved. I'm truly honoured and thankful for your offer and support. Let's do this." They continued toward the hideout Marilyn had described; it was a further thirteen miles. Marilyn reached across, took Darcy's hand from the steering wheel, and gave it a small, steady squeeze before letting it fall back into her lap, where Marilyn folded her hands together, still and resolute. In that precise moment, Darcy realised that Marilyn and the group she represented would be part of her life for a very long time, assuming she survived this first mission.

Chapter 11

Marilyn told Darcy to pull over to the right-hand side of the main road they had been travelling on and turn onto a rough, uneven street. Stones scattered in all directions under the tyres as the car bumped along before emerging into a wide, open space where six other vehicles were parked, mostly 4x4s. The area was desolate, save for one substantial warehouse standing directly ahead of them.

The surroundings were eerily empty, no street lamps, no greenery, not even a telegraph pole in sight. Just the lone building, encircled by distant mountains on every side. Well hidden, Darcy thought.

Although the warehouse looked fairly new, she could tell it was decades old and had likely undergone extensive renovation on the outside. That thought prompted her to ask, "How is this group funded?"

Marilyn smiled, her brilliant white teeth contrasting with her tanned complexion. "We're not funded at all. We keep ourselves completely anonymous and have all agreed to carry out our missions voluntarily. This is what we live for, you can't put a price on that. What matters to us, we give our time and money to."

Darcy could feel the compassion radiating from Marilyn, an energy so strong it seemed to envelop her. A lump formed in her throat, and tears welled in her eyes. In that moment, she felt she might burst, overwhelmed by gratitude and warmth for this woman. She had never met anyone like Marilyn and knew in her heart that she was an angel sent to her at exactly the right time.

Darcy couldn't find the words. She simply smiled and threw her arms around Marilyn, holding her tightly. The only words she managed to stammer out were, "Thank you so much for everything. I'm honoured to have met you, I'll never forget you."

Marilyn's own eyes filled with tears, one escaping down her left cheek. Taking a deep breath, she replied softly, "Don't thank me just yet, we're only just beginning. But you're very welcome. I know for sure we'll be friends for a very long time."

They both composed themselves, wiping away their stray tears, before stepping out of the car and walking the short distance to the warehouse entrance.

Marilyn typed a numbered code into the keypad beside the door. A green light flashed, and the heavy metal door swung open with a mechanical click. Darcy stepped in behind her, closing it firmly. Directly ahead was a set of concrete stairs, and to the right, a narrow hallway led to another door but Marilyn didn't hesitate. She took Darcy's hand and headed up the stairs.

They climbed two flights before reaching the top, where Darcy suddenly felt her nerves take over. Her chest tightened at the thought of who she was about to meet. Marilyn sensed her tension, gave her a quick reassuring hug, and mouthed, "Relax. It's all okay."

They stepped into a vast open space, a striking contrast to the industrial exterior. The interior was beautifully designed, with sleek, modern furniture and spotlights illuminating the concrete walls. Along the far side, a kitchen had been built into an exposed brick wall of varying earthy tones, giving the whole place a warm, contemporary feel. It's beautiful, Darcy thought. I'd love my home to look like this.

She scanned the room and the sofas were empty, and there was no one in the kitchen or at the large wooden table.

Peering cautiously around a partitioned wall, she froze in amazement. Before her stood a glass-panelled room filled with computers, tangled cables, and high-tech equipment. A large conference table and leather chairs filled the centre, and a massive screen covered the far wall. Everything about the setup screamed mission control.

Inside were eleven people, men and women alike, all dressed in black cargo trousers, fitted T-shirts, and padded vests. Every outfit was practical, bristling with hidden pockets for gear and tools. As soon as they noticed Marilyn, the serious expressions on their faces softened into warm smiles.

One by one, they stood and greeted her with hugs and quiet words of welcome before turning to shake Darcy's hand. Each introduced themselves in turn: Dan, Matt, Laura, Rachel, Harmony, Robbie, Cal, Danny, Leo, Rio, and Giuseppe. They looked formidable, a force to be reckoned with, yet Darcy could feel a kindness beneath their hardened exteriors, a shared compassion that made her instantly trust them.

Her attention was drawn to a large board mounted on the wall. From the detailed notes and images, Darcy realised

Marilyn must have briefed the team during their drive, though she couldn't recall the conversation herself, she had been too lost in her thoughts, overwhelmed by disbelief at the depth of help these strangers were offering.

Pinned at the centre of the board was a photograph of the building they would soon confront, the so-called psychiatric hospital. The image made Darcy's stomach twist. The paintwork was a lifeless grey, the windows cracked and splintered in places, their frames crumbling with decay. The surrounding trees and plants did little to soften its bleakness. To her, it looked like something straight out of a horror film, a place of suffering and secrets that should have been demolished long ago.

Darcy didn't want to look at the board any longer, yet she couldn't tear her eyes away from it. Surrounding the central photograph of the hospital were eight smaller images, each capturing different individuals entering or leaving the building at various times. Darcy assumed they were accomplices of the trafficking network, the perpetrators of the unimaginable abuse happening within those walls. The thought made her stomach turn. Beads of sweat formed along her hairline, trickling down her face and neck. She needed air, now.

Bolting from the room, she tore down the stairs, slammed her hand against the door release button, and burst outside. The cold air hit her like a wave. She dropped to her knees on the rough, stony ground, buried her face in her hands, and sobbed until there were no tears left.

A faint sound of footsteps approached from behind. Strong, warm arms wrapped around her shoulders. She looked up into the face of a man, Danny, she thought. It would take her some time to learn all their names. She didn't even know if their group had a name. What she did know was how genuinely compassionate these people were.

She let the embrace linger for a moment before rising unsteadily to her feet. Turning to face him, she managed a weary smile and thanked him for his kindness, nodding that she was ready to return and face the board once more.

Danny hesitated, then asked gently, "May I ask why you're wearing sunglasses and a scarf indoors? I can understand the cap, but the rest?"

Only then did Darcy realise she was still wearing them, she'd been so caught up in the introductions, the shock of the photographs, and the overwhelming reality of the mission that she hadn't even thought to remove them.

"Oh, I don't usually wear these," she replied, embarrassed. "Certainly not indoors. But I needed a disguise, something to keep me off any CCTV. It's just in case things get complicated later when it comes to finding my sister. I'd rather keep my involvement quiet. Does that make sense? I don't really trust many people, especially those in authority who are meant to protect us."

Danny nodded in understanding. "Yeah," he said quietly. "Makes sense."

As they climbed the stairs back to the operations room, an image flashed in Darcy's mind, the haunting face of her sister, aged and weary. She was certain she had seen Faith's photograph pinned to that board before she fled the room.

Chapter 12

Darcy suddenly felt an overwhelming urge to rush back up the concrete stairs. She stumbled on the last step in her haste and froze as soon as she reached the board. There it was, the photo that had stopped her heart.

She stood motionless for what felt like an eternity, staring at the image. The woman's face was drawn, hollow, and gaunt, almost unrecognisable, but Darcy knew. Beneath the exhaustion and despair, she could see the faint trace of the smile that once lit her sister's features. The photograph showed Faith being dragged into the building by a large man, his grip firm around her arm as he pulled her inside.

Rage and sorrow boiled within Darcy, threatening to tear her apart. She didn't know what to do with the grief that consumed her. She turned to Danny and mouthed silently, That's my sister. No sound escaped her lips. But Danny understood, his expression softened, and a sheen of tears formed in his eyes as he gave her a quiet, affirming nod.

Darcy struggled to face anyone's sympathy; compassion always made her feel raw and exposed. She deflected it the only way she knew how. "Do you have a boxing bag anywhere in the building?" she asked, her voice strained.

Danny quickly composed himself. "Of course we do," he said. "It was one of the first things we insisted on having here."

He led her to a large open space at the back of the building, a fully equipped gym with every machine and piece of equipment any fitness enthusiast could dream of. Without hesitation, Darcy went straight to the heavy punching bag. She slipped her hands into a pair of oversized gloves lying nearby and began to hit the bag with everything she had.

Every strike carried the weight of her pain, every memory, every unanswered question, every year she had lived without her sisters. Her fists pounded against the leather with such force that it was a wonder the chains held.

Danny stood silently in the corner, arms folded, watching her with quiet admiration. He knew this was more than anger, it was a lifetime of love and loss finding its release.

Danny could see Darcy's strength and determination,

but he couldn't help wondering whether this mission might ultimately break her completely. Though he had quickly begun to understand her disposition, he still didn't truly know her, not the full extent of what she was capable of, either mentally or physically. He could only hope that when all of this was over, whatever the outcome, Darcy's soul would remain whole and not lost or shattered beyond repair.

He watched her for nearly twenty minutes, relentlessly pounding the boxing bag until it seemed ready to burst. Finally, he called out, "Okay, I think we should both grab some drinks before you burn out and collapse."

Darcy paused reluctantly, then let the gloves drop to the floor. She bent forward, catching her breath, before joining Danny for the short walk to the kitchen. He grabbed two bottles of water from the fridge, gestured for her to take the seat opposite him at the table, and encouraged her to talk about what she was feeling.

At first, Darcy didn't want to speak. She didn't want to do anything. Her thoughts were a jumble of anger, grief, and impulsive resolve, a voice in her head urging her to storm the building and drag her sister out herself, consequences be damned. But deep down, she knew that was reckless. Instead, she forced herself to open up, something she rarely did. She didn't often trust people, especially with her emotion, but there was something about Danny's calm, empathetic presence that made her feel safe enough to try.

Slowly, she began to talk, about her life before and after her sisters' abductions, about the endless nights of searching and despair, about how surprised she was to still be standing after everything. She admitted that her sole purpose in life had been to bring her sister's home, though now she only had the chance to save one.

Danny didn't interrupt once. He sat silently, listening, giving her the space to release years of pain that had been locked inside. When Darcy finally ran out of words, she exhaled deeply and looked up at him, expecting to find the same look of sympathy she had seen earlier.

To her surprise, Danny was smiling. Confused, she frowned slightly, but before she could speak, he said softly, "I'm not smiling out of pity. I'm smiling because I'm grateful you shared that with me, and because it's inspiring. You've been through so much, yet you're still standing, still hopeful. That kind of love and strength… it's rare. Hold onto it. It's what will get you through."

Danny felt it was only fair to reciprocate by sharing his own story, the reason he had joined the group. Clearing his throat, he began softly, "I feel honoured to be part of this team, this very special group. I truly believe in what we're trying to achieve every day: to bring loved ones home and to get justice for families who've already lost so much.

"My little girl, Lila, went missing a year ago. She was three. I wouldn't still be alive if it weren't for this group of amazing, selfless people. Lila was my world, my everything. I never got to bring her home. Instead, I got to bury her." He paused, his voice faltering. "And as painful as that was, I suppose it's something, because not everyone gets that closure in the end.

"We caught the vile gang that took her, but even that didn't bring her back. These brutal operations happen every single day, everywhere. That's why I do this, why we all do. Our role is to help rescue those who've been taken and, hopefully, to stop this evil altogether. It takes an enormous effort, people, time, resources, but day by day, we're making a difference. We're helping as many as we can, and we're spreading the word, encouraging more groups like ours across the world.

"If it takes another ten years, or even longer, then so be it. My only reason for carrying on is knowing that my Lila would have wanted me to do the same, to help other families bring their children back home."

Darcy couldn't respond at first. She sat in silence, absorbing every word. The weight of his pain was overwhelming; she couldn't begin to imagine the sorrow he had endured, and was still enduring. His beautiful little girl. The thought alone made her chest tighten.

Quietly, Darcy reached across the table and took Danny's hand. Looking into his tear-streaked face, she murmured, "I'm truly so, so sorry."

Danny wiped his eyes with the back of his free hand and managed a faint smile. "You've nothing to be sorry for," he said softly. "Thank you for your kind words, and for listening. I think I'll rest for a bit. Let's meet in the conference room at five to plan for tonight. I'll let the others know."

Darcy nodded in agreement and released his hand. Danny rose slowly from the table and walked wearily out of the kitchen, heading towards the sleeping quarters on the upper level.

Once he was gone, Darcy buried her face in her hands and began to cry again, this time for a man she had only just met, and for a daughter she would never know. She couldn't believe how much pain and loss these brave, beautiful people had endured, yet they still found the strength to keep fighting.

Wiping her tears, Darcy made herself a silent promise, she would make sure more groups like this one were formed, not just across the country but around the world. After a few minutes of reflection, she decided to rest. She knew she would need her strength for the mission ahead.

She lay down on the sofa in the recreation room, set her alarm for 4:30 p.m., and closed her eyes. As she drifted into deep meditation, she sent her thoughts outward, asking the questions that had burned inside her for far too long, hoping for the guidance she so desperately needed.

Chapter 13

Darcy woke with a start, jolted by Marilyn's gentle hand shaking her shoulder. Disoriented, she blinked rapidly, trying to recall where she was. Marilyn's calm voice broke through the fog. "You were having a nightmare," she said softly. "I thought it best to wake you before you fell off the sofa."

Darcy sat up, visibly shaken, fragments of her dream flooding back. She had seen Penelope's face, terrified, pleading for help, and then Faith, clutching at her arms, begging her to save her before a masked figure dragged her away. Her chest tightened as panic rose, but she forced herself to take quick breaths followed by long, steady inhales until the trembling subsided.

"Thank you," she said quietly, looking apologetically at Marilyn.

"There's no need to apologise," Marilyn replied gently. "You must be exhausted, your body and mind are in overdrive. Why don't you get some proper rest upstairs in a real bed? Maybe have a shot of something strong to help you sleep. We'll handle the recon and update you once you've had some rest."

Darcy wanted nothing more than to plan her sister's rescue, but she knew Marilyn was right. She wouldn't be any use to Faith if she collapsed from exhaustion. Nodding in reluctant agreement, she followed Marilyn upstairs to a small vacant room with a single camp bed that looked surprisingly comfortable.

"Don't set an alarm," Marilyn instructed. "I'll wake you myself in a few hours. I don't know when you last slept, but you definitely need it. Here, have this shot of vodka and settle down."

She crossed the room to close the curtains, shutting out the last streaks of sunlight, then left quietly, closing the door behind her.

Darcy downed the vodka in one gulp, anything to still her mind. The warmth of the drink spread through her chest as she lay back on the bed. The scent of freshly washed bedding filled the room, bringing back memories of home, of nights when clean sheets and calm thoughts were enough to make her feel safe. The familiarity soothed her. Her eyelids grew heavy, and before long, she drifted into deep sleep.

Several hours later, she woke to a soft tapping and her name spoken in Marilyn's soothing voice. Groggy but comforted, Darcy instinctively reached up and hugged her. The sudden gesture made Marilyn gasp, her eyes widening in surprise before she smiled and returned the embrace.

They stayed like that for a few moments, no words needed, their mutual understanding speaking louder than anything either could say.

When they finally pulled apart, Darcy immediately launched into a rush of questions. "Has the meeting taken place? What was the outcome? What's the plan? Are we all heading out tonight?"

Marilyn held up her hands. "Whoa, with all the questions. Take a breath. Yes, the meeting's finished, and we've obtained the building's infrastructure details. From the photographs we've gathered, we're confident in our plan to travel there tonight and observe."

Darcy wanted more, she wanted to storm the place that very night. "We need to get in and out tonight, Marilyn. It needs to happen now, it needs to…" she began, voice rising.

Marilyn cut her off, firm. "No, Darcy. We must carry out this plan methodically and properly, not rush in without the necessary information. We'll split into groups: two cars with four people each, and one car with five. We'll record the comings and goings of everyone involved and tally the number of victims held. We'll observe over three nights and then move in. If we act now without proper planning and intel, we'll all be in danger, and there will be no successful rescues. Do you want that?" Her tone was stern but threaded with compassion.

Darcy understood. She realised she had to slow down and compartmentalise. This was a mission involving twelve other dedicated people, all there to help her and Faith. She could not let panic drive the operation, she must not be the weak link. Apologising, she told Marilyn she didn't want a failed mission that would put everyone at risk, and she agreed to attend tonight's first observation.

Marilyn suggested Darcy take a well-earned shower and reheat the pasta she'd prepared an hour earlier. Darcy thanked her for the food and the group's support, then headed to the bathroom. She lingered under the hot water for half an hour, letting it pour over her aching, tired body. Showers usually washed her worries away, but this time the relief didn't last, if anything, the anxiety returned stronger. Her nerves were taut with the anticipation of the first observation and the remote possibility of seeing her sister from afar. She knew that was unlikely, but she feared seeing the faces of the monsters who held Faith and perhaps many others. The thought made her shiver.

She dressed in clean clothes from her rucksack, brushed her teeth, applied moisturiser to her dry skin, and made her way downstairs.

All twelve members were gathered in the recreation room, chatting and going over the upcoming plans. They each greeted Darcy with a warm "Hello." Danny offered to eat with her, he hadn't had a proper meal yet, and she accepted. They made their way to the kitchen area and ate together, making light conversation and feeling comfortable in one another's company. Darcy felt she could tell Danny anything; it was as if she had known him for years.

During her earlier meditation, before she finally slept, she had seen Danny and been told he was part of her family in a previous lifetime, that their souls had met again in this life to help one another and form a lasting friendship. Darcy had recognised that truth the moment she first met him, just as she had when she first met Marilyn. These meetings felt meant to be, at least in her reality. The meditation had also answered many questions she'd been carrying about Faith and the impending mission, and the relief she felt was immense.

Shortly after dinner they collected the necessary equipment, climbed into the vehicles and set off towards the hospital. Each car took up the positions they had agreed on and prepared for the night's observation.

Chapter 14

Darcy and the group, which she now learned called themselves the Merkaba, were devoted to bringing balance and harmony to the world, or at least to as many people as was humanly possible. Over three consecutive nights, they carried out their observations. By the end, Darcy and her new friends were utterly exhausted, sickened and horrified by what they had witnessed.

Some of the men entering and leaving the building were well-dressed and freshly shaven, their smug expressions suggesting a sense of superiority. There were women too, some accompanying the men, others alone, all equally immaculate and self-assured. Then there were the others: men in tracksuits and even some in combat gear, their presence completely out of place for an establishment posing as a hospital.

On the second night, the team observed women and children being escorted into the building. On the third night, only some of those same women and children emerged. The despair in their body language, the emptiness in their faces, and the state of their clothing were unbearable to witness. It took every ounce of restraint for the group not to intervene. Darcy kept pleading, "What are we waiting for? Let's go now!" But her friends held her back, reminding her that acting too soon would jeopardise everything, if they rushed in without proper planning, they could lose their lives and fail the very people they were trying to save.

Eventually, Darcy forced herself to calm down. She understood that patience was vital, even though it went against every instinct she had. Still, sitting in that car for hours on end, powerless to act, took every bit of her strength.

On the final night of observation, they drove back to the warehouse in complete silence. The air inside the vehicles was thick with sorrow and frustration. When they arrived, no one spoke a word. One by one, each member trudged upstairs and disappeared into their rooms without eating a thing.

Darcy was physically and emotionally drained. She lay down on her bed still in her day clothes, trying to push away the faces of the victims, and the survivors, that haunted her thoughts. But the images wouldn't leave her.

Then another thought struck her like a knife: in all three nights of surveillance, she hadn't seen her sister once.

Not entering, not leaving. The idea hit hard, perhaps Faith had been moved elsewhere before the observations even began. The possibility gnawed at her.

Unable to quiet her racing mind, she whispered a plea to her divine team, asking if her sister was still inside the building. For a long moment, there was only silence, and then the lightbulb above her flickered once, twice, before returning to steady glow. Darcy took it as her sign: yes, Faith was still there.

She didn't dare ask if her sister was alive, she wasn't ready for that answer. Turning onto her front, she buried her face into the pillow and let the tears flow until exhaustion finally pulled her into sleep.

Darcy woke at 6 a.m., shaken from a grisly nightmare in which she too had been trapped inside that ghastly building. She couldn't shake the feeling that it might have been a premonition. Determined to ground herself, she stepped into the shower. The warm water soothed her skin, washing away the remnants of fear and exhaustion. She took it as a cleansing, an energy clearing, and when she emerged, she felt more like herself, whatever that meant these days.

After dressing in clean clothes, she felt grateful she

had packed enough for the journey. Unsure whether anyone else would be awake so early, she made her way downstairs, and was surprised to find everyone already up.

All twelve were in the kitchen, some gathered around the breakfast bar, others at the table. Rio, Giuseppe, Cal, Harmony and Rachel were busily sharing the cooking duties. Rio and Giuseppe handled the eggs and cheese; Harmony and Cal worked on the muffins and waffles; and Rachel tended to the fruit and syrup. Their laughter and chatter filled the room, a rare sound after the grim nights they had endured. The scene was a welcome change, and Darcy found herself smiling at the warmth and normality of it. She knew that before long, such moments would be replaced by the horrors awaiting them inside the so-called hospital. She vowed to savour this one.

Robbie waved her over to take the seat beside him at the breakfast bar. Easy-going and cheeky, he had a mischievous grin that was hard not to return. Darcy realised she knew little of the others' personal stories, beyond Danny's and snippets of Marilyn's, and decided it was best to let people share in their own time.

She couldn't help but wonder where she would be if

she hadn't met Marilyn. Probably dead, she thought grimly, before shaking off the notion and focusing on Robbie.

He was still smiling, asking what she fancied for breakfast, or if she wanted a bit of everything. "How are you feeling?" he added gently. "Any worries about tonight?"

Darcy chose eggs and cheese with muffins, hoping she'd be able to keep the food down. "I'm feeling anxious," she admitted. "And a bit sick, to be honest. I might go for a run later to clear my head, release some tension."

"That's completely normal," Robbie said reassuringly. "Everyone feels that way before a mission. I'll come with you, company helps."

Darcy smiled gratefully. "I'd like that."

Laura, overhearing, piped up from across the room. "Mind if I join you two?"

"Of course not," Robbie replied, glancing at Darcy, who nodded in agreement.

The three of them exchanged knowing smiles, a small spark of camaraderie before the storm.

After a hearty breakfast, tasty, if not entirely settling

on Darcy's tense stomach, everyone gathered in the conference room. The plan was reviewed in detail: roles were assigned, positions within and around the building clarified, and timings confirmed for the evening's operation. Each member of Merkaba appeared confident in their role and how to execute the plan; Darcy felt the opposite. This was not her world or routine, though she hoped, if all went well, to continue working with the group long after tonight. She checked her kit and made sure her taser was packed.

After the briefing, Darcy went for a run with Robbie and Laura, then did a short boxing session on her return. A hot shower followed, and she dressed in the kit she had prepared, checking every piece of equipment once more. Back in the conference room the team ran through their checks together, swapping gear, confirming radios, and going over the plan one last time.

At 8 p.m. they left in four vehicles and parked in their designated positions. They would observe the site for two hours and, once they were confident all was still and quiet, begin the operation at 10 p.m.

Chapter 15

They watched the last man enter the building at 9:45 p.m. and waited a further forty-five minutes to ensure no one else went inside. At 10:30 p.m., they made their move. In three groups, they left their vehicles and approached from different directions, one team through the back entrance, another via the fire exit on the side, and the final group through the main front door.

Before they entered, Robbie cut the power supply, plunging the building into darkness. Each member slipped on their night-vision goggles from the backpacks they'd prepared back at the warehouse.

Darcy joined Marilyn, Danny, Laura, and Cal. Her stomach tightened; this was her first experience of anything like this. Still, the intense training she'd undergone during her time with Merkaba had prepared her well. The others offered quiet reassurance, gentle pats on the shoulder, quick nods of confidence. They reminded her they had her back.

Darcy's main focus was clear: find Faith. But as she crept forward, she couldn't ignore the thought of the other women and children trapped inside. She knew she would help with their rescue too, yet for now, she needed to concentrate on one task at a time. First Faith. Then the others.

She was the last to slip through the side entrance, the heavy door clanging shut behind her. The sound echoed through the corridor, setting her nerves on edge. Adjusting the side clip on her goggles, she blinked until the view sharpened.

In her right hand, she held a truncheon; in her left, her taser. Two metres of rope and several zip ties were tucked into her backpack, along with other essentials. A canister of pepper spray rested in the front pocket of her combat jacket, her fingers already curled around the top, ready for use.

She followed closely behind her group, her movements careful and deliberate. The corridor was long and narrow, lined with walls coated in peeling paint that curled and flaked with age. Cobwebs hung thickly in the corners, and patches of damp spread across the walls like a dark, mouldy map. Cracked skirting boards had started to detach, and the tiled floor beneath her boots was uneven and filthy, worn from decades of neglect.

Darcy kept her head low to avoid tripping, glancing up and down every few seconds, a rhythm of vigilance, each step taking her deeper into the unknown.

The scene felt as though it had been lifted straight from a horror film. Every instinct in Darcy's body screamed at her to turn and run, but she knew she couldn't, not now. She had to push through the fear for her sister.

Without warning, a door on the right burst open. A grisly-looking man, short and thickset with a completely shaved head, stumbled out into the corridor and slammed straight into Danny, throwing him hard against the opposite wall.

Darcy's heart leapt. She spotted a handgun tucked into the back pocket of the man's jeans and moved instinctively towards him, desperate to disarm him before he reached for it. But Cal had already seen it. Moving with lightning speed, he lunged forward and brought the man crashing down onto the grimy, hard floor. In a matter of seconds, Cal had restrained him, zip-tying his wrists behind his back, binding his ankles tightly with rope, and stuffing a rag into his mouth to keep him silent.

Darcy stood frozen for a heartbeat, both impressed and startled by Cal's swift reaction, but her focus quickly shifted to Danny. He had managed to pull himself away from the wall, though a swelling had already begun to rise on his left cheek and a thin stream of blood trickled down from a gash near his temple.

She hurried over, fumbling through her backpack, her night-vision goggles still in place. Her shaking hands found the first aid kit. Pulling out gauze and a bandage, she carefully wiped away the blood with an antiseptic wipe, then pressed the gauze over the cut and secured it tightly with the bandage.

Danny winced but managed a faint smile. "Thanks," he murmured.

"Don't move too quickly," Darcy whispered, still worried that the injury might worsen later.

"I'm fine," Danny said quietly, though his voice wavered slightly.

Meanwhile, Cal and Laura dragged the subdued man back into the room he'd come from. Inside, the flickering glow of a television illuminated the dingy space, it was still playing what looked like a video game. Rachel walked over and switched it off, plunging the room into shadow.

There wasn't much else inside, just a small table, a single chair, a half-eaten plate of food, and the man's mobile phone lying beside it. The ordinariness of it all only made the place feel more sinister.

They moved the restrained man to the back of the room, where he lay slumped against the wall, still unconscious. Laura retrieved his phone from the table and slipped it into her back pocket. With the door shut tightly behind them, the group continued down the dim corridor until they reached four more doors, two on either side.

Each of them pressed an ear against a door, listening intently. Nothing. Not a sound came from within any of the rooms. Rachel gestured silently that she would stand guard while the others checked each one in turn.

The group eased open the creaking doors, weapons at the ready. Darcy unclipped her truncheon from her belt and swapped it for her taser, then pulled the pepper spray from her jacket pocket, holding it out in front of her at arm's length. Her pulse thundered in her ears as she inched the door open wider and peered around the frame.

Before she could react, a face appeared from the darkness, a man lunging at her from just inside the doorway. Darcy acted on pure instinct, pressing down hard on the spray. The stream hit him squarely in the eyes. He howled in pain, stumbling backwards and clutching at his face.

Darcy kicked out, connecting sharply with the back of his knee. The man crumpled forward, hitting the filthy floor. She aimed her taser, fired, and watched as the electric current jolted through his body for several seconds before he went limp.

She took a deep breath, the adrenaline pounding through her. But she didn't hear the second man.

Before she could turn, a pair of rough hands yanked her backwards by the hair, dragging her into the centre of the room. She barely had time to gasp before a brutal punch connected squarely with her nose. A sharp crack echoed in her ears, bone splitting, followed by the slam of the door.

Then everything went dark.

Chapter 16

"Wake up, wake up, wake up."

That was all Darcy could hear echoing inside her pounding head. Her face throbbed, the skin around her eyes swollen and tight; she could barely lift her eyelids. She lay still, forcing herself to listen for any sound in the darkness. Her night-vision goggles were gone, she could feel the cool air on her face, and she didn't dare move, unsure who might be in the room with her. The last thing she wanted was another blow… or something far worse.

Pain pulsed through every part of her body. Her nose felt broken; her whole body was on high alert, every nerve buzzing and tingling as though electricity ran through her veins. She feared she might faint again.

Closing her eyes, she tried to steady her breathing and reach for her inner voice, the familiar guidance of her spirit team. For a moment, there was only silence. Then, clear as day, a voice came through:

"You are okay. You will heal. But you need to get

up, now. We are here with you. Muster all your strength and get up, NOW!"

Her eyes flickered open just as she heard scurrying footsteps moving rapidly across the floor. Someone was beside her, closing in. In an instant, something heavy pressed down on her chest, trying to pin her. Panic surged when she realised her hands were tied behind her back.

She couldn't think, only act. Gathering every ounce of strength, Darcy twisted her body violently and threw her full weight sideways. Whoever was on top of her lost balance and crashed to the floor. She gritted her teeth against the pain and forced her eyes open.

Through the blur and dim light, she recognised the face of the same horrendous man who had attacked her earlier. She had no idea how much time had passed, minutes, hours, but she knew she couldn't give him another chance.

He began to rise to his knees, but Darcy reacted first. She pulled both legs up and kicked out hard, her boots slamming into his chest. He gasped, staggering backwards, and before he could recover, she kicked again, this time connecting with his face. The man fell back with a heavy thud, his head cracking against the cold stone floor. Then he went still.

Darcy sat up as far as the bindings allowed, panting, heart hammering in her chest. She knew she had little time before he regained consciousness, or worse, before someone else came in.

Her eyes adjusted slowly to the gloom. The room was small, windowless, and oppressively silent, almost identical to the one she had entered earlier. The same cracked walls, the same rank smell of damp and decay.

The room was bare, with only a few pieces of old furniture. The floor was cold and uneven, and in one corner, a small sink clung to the wall, perhaps a remnant from when the building truly had been a hospital. Darcy's immediate priority was to free her hands, but her pocket knife was tucked away in the front pocket of her trousers, completely out of reach.

She scanned the room desperately for something sharp, anything that could cut through the ties, but there was nothing useful in sight. The stench of damp and decay filled the air, turning her stomach. She needed to get out, quickly. She didn't want to think about what the man might do to her if he woke before she escaped, but the memory of him trying to climb on top of her told her enough.

Drawing on the strength and flexibility she had gained from her training with Merkaba, Darcy began to manoeuvre her body. She bent her knees slightly, trying to wriggle her arms down towards her feet, but her balance gave way and she toppled sideways onto the floor. Gritting her teeth, she tried again, this time remaining on her side for better leverage. Inch by inch, she managed to bring her arms lower until her bound hands reached her heels. With one final twist, she pulled her arms over her feet and up towards her chest.

Panting from the effort, Darcy reached into her trouser pocket and hooked the small knife around her index finger. She twisted it into her right hand and, with careful precision, began sawing through the plastic ties around her wrists. After a few tense seconds, the last strand snapped. She was free.

She quickly patted down her pockets, all empty. Her heart sank. Scanning the shadowy room, she searched for her missing weapons and phone but saw nothing. Crossing to the unconscious man, she knelt beside him and checked his pockets. Relief washed over her when she found her mobile, but none of her other equipment was there.

The room was pitch dark without power. The only trace of light came from a narrow crack at the edge of a boarded-up window, where a faint orange glow from a street lamp bled through. The dim light was barely enough to make out the outlines of furniture or the man's motionless body.

Darcy felt her way along a small table to her left, hoping to find her night-vision goggles, but her fingers met only dust and splinters. Her torch was in her backpack too, likely confiscated along with the rest of her gear. It would have been invaluable right now.

At that precise moment, she heard the faint click of the door unlocking. Darcy froze where she stood. Her breath quickened, her heartbeat thudding so loudly she was sure it would give her away. Every sense heightened — sound, smell, instinct — all on alert.

A familiar mix of body odour and cologne drifted through the doorway. Her mind raced as recognition flickered. Danny. It smelled like Danny. Relief surged through her chest, but she dared not assume. She had to be certain.

Dropping into a crouch, Darcy stayed as low and still as possible, every muscle tensed. The silence stretched until her inner voice finally broke through the noise in her mind, whispering softly, You are safe now.

A sudden beam of light cut through the darkness, blinding her for a moment. The torchlight hit her square in the face, making her squint as she tried to focus on the figure in the doorway.

Then came the voice — warm, steady, unmistakable.

"Are you just going to kneel there," Danny said, "or do you want to get out of here?"

Chapter 17

The emotions that surged through Darcy at that moment were indescribable. Relief, disbelief, gratitude — all at once. It felt as though her heart might burst from her chest. She ran to Danny and threw her arms around him, holding him so tightly that he let out a strained laugh.

"Okay, okay," he gasped, half-laughing, half-breathless. "You can put me down now. I'm so thankful you're alright. Apart from what looks like a broken nose and a very swollen face, you don't seem too badly hurt. Did that man do anything else to you? Please tell me if he did — I swear, if he did, I might not be able to control myself."

Darcy shook her head quickly, reassuring him. "No, I managed to stop him before he could… but he wanted to. I could feel it."

Danny's expression hardened. He strode over to the unconscious man and, with the green glow of his night-vision goggles illuminating his movements, retrieved a syringe from his backpack. He knelt beside the attacker, pushed the needle into the man's arm, and depressed the plunger.

Darcy frowned. "What did you just inject him with?"

"Just a sedative," Danny replied calmly. "It'll keep him under until the police arrive — though we've also alerted the agencies, just in case. We're still not sure who in the force we can trust."

Darcy's stomach tightened. "Wait — the police? You've called them already?" Her voice rose slightly. "Danny, I haven't found my sister yet! Have you found the women and children?"

Danny turned towards her and handed over her night-vision goggles. As she adjusted them back into place, the full picture came into view — and with it, the look on Danny's face. His expression was drawn and weary, his eyes red-rimmed.

"We've found some," he said quietly, his voice breaking. "But not all. From the photos we gathered before the mission, six children and three women are still unaccounted for — your sister among them."

He turned away, hiding his face as his shoulders shook. "We've cleared the ground floor. That's where most of the men were — eleven in total. They've all been taken down and sedated; they won't wake for at least two hours. We've secured this level completely. Next, we move upstairs to finish the search. We'll contact the police and the agencies after we've rescued everyone. We can't risk interference until it's done."

He paused, his voice tightening. "Darcy… it's horrific. The things we've seen. The way these people have been living — what they've endured. No one deserves that." He looked directly into her eyes. "Are you ready to find your sister?"

Before she could answer, Danny's radio crackled with static, followed by a clear voice echoing through the silence.

"We've gained entry to six rooms on the upper level," Marilyn's voice came through, professional yet trembling. "Three more children and two women have been located. Two guards were positioned upstairs — both neutralised and sedated. No other rooms visible. How should we proceed?"

Her tone was steady, but Darcy could hear it — the faint edge of sadness, the unspoken realisation that Faith was still missing.

Darcy's mind was spinning with a thousand thoughts. How could her sister have vanished? It didn't make sense. Faith couldn't have been moved during their observations — not without being seen. Cameras had been placed discreetly at every angle of the property: the sides, the back, the front. There was no way that Faith, along with the three remaining children, could simply disappear without being caught on camera.

Something was missing. Something hidden.

Darcy's pulse quickened as her thoughts aligned. A basement. Of course. An old psychiatric hospital would almost certainly have one — somewhere beneath, sealed away from the world. She turned sharply to Danny, her voice trembling with urgency.

"There has to be a basement, or at least a hidden room somewhere — on one of the levels!"

Danny's eyes widened. Without hesitation, he lifted his radio and spoke into it, his voice firm.

"Everyone, listen up. Check for anything that doesn't look like a standard door — hidden panels, floor hatches, anything. Darcy and I will search for signs of a basement. It's not on the blueprints, but that doesn't mean it isn't there. Stay alert."

With that, they both sprang into action. Grabbing their backpacks, they sprinted down the corridor, turning into an adjoining passageway, their torches flickering against the cracked and grimy walls. They ran their hands along every surface, feeling for irregularities — anything that might reveal a concealed opening.

Then Darcy felt it — a tingling sensation that started at the crown of her head and coursed down to her stomach. It was the unmistakable sign she always felt when her guides were trying to tell her something. She stopped, breathing deeply, scanning her surroundings.

To her left, a patch of wall caught her attention. The paint there looked different — thicker, uneven, and oddly textured compared to the rest. She shone her torch directly on it, and through her goggles, the area appeared to be a darker shade than the wall around it.

Suddenly, a faint white beam of light appeared, circling the patch of wall in smooth, glowing loops. Darcy blinked hard, unsure if this was real or something only she could see.

"Danny… can you see that?" she whispered.

"See what?" he replied, glancing over. "I don't see anything."

Before she could respond, nine butterflies — radiant and ethereal, in shades of blue, gold, and violet — emerged, fluttering gracefully around the patch of wall. Their delicate wings shimmered in the dim light. Darcy didn't ask Danny again; she already knew he couldn't see them.

Her heart filled with certainty. The butterflies were her sign. Her spirit guides were showing her the way — this wall was hiding something.

"Danny, it's here," she said quietly but with conviction. "This is the entry point. There's something behind this wall."

They began feeling along the surface, searching carefully. Then Darcy's fingers brushed against something small and metallic — a round button, almost invisible beneath a layer of painted plaster. She crouched down, placed her torch on the floor so that it illuminated the wall, and gripped her pepper spray in one hand and her taser in the other.

She looked at Danny, who stood close beside her, weapon ready.

"Here goes," she whispered, pressing the button.

The door silently opened inwards revealing a set of concrete steps leading to the basement. They both turned to each other with smirks on their faces, Darcy grabbing her torch off the floor and made her way down the steps with Danny following behind.

Chapter 18

Darcy crept down the steep steps, watching out for anything that could trip her up. At the bottom, she turned cautiously to the left, feeling Danny's hand rest reassuringly on her shoulder. His touch brought a fleeting sense of comfort and safety, though her heart was pounding with anticipation. She had no idea what to expect around that corner.

Suddenly, a sharp beam of light cut through her night-vision goggles, forcing her to rip them off. As her eyes adjusted, she was met by the flickering glow of a single candle in the corner of the room. Turning away from the light, her gaze fell upon two single mattresses laid side by side on the bare concrete floor. Scattered around them were items of mismatched clothing in dull colours, along with baby bottles and nappies. A foul stench of body odour and soiled nappies hung in the air, making Darcy's stomach tighten.

Her eyes followed the outline of the mattresses to a heap of blankets draped across them. Then, to her horror, she noticed the blankets shifting ever so slightly—rising and falling in a slow rhythm. Her breath caught, her pulse racing as she realised there was someone—perhaps more than one person—beneath them.

Her hands began to tremble violently, and she panted as she moved closer. Danny's hand tightened on her shoulder, silently urging her to stop, but she ignored him and continued forward. Behind her, she heard him draw his weapon. With her heart hammering in her chest, Darcy reached for the blanket's edge and yanked it back in one swift motion.

What she saw made her freeze. Lying before her, staring up with eyes wide with fear and confusion, was her sister Faith—and beside her, a small baby boy, no more than four months old, smiling up at the candlelight.

Darcy gasped and fell to her knees, pulling Faith into her arms. The frailness of her sister's body shocked her. Faith, once so vibrant and strong, now looked at least four stone lighter—her face gaunt, her frame skeletal. But when Faith's deep blue eyes finally recognised the woman holding her, they filled with tears and disbelief. She could hardly comprehend that her sister had truly found her after all this time.

Faith had always known that Darcy would never stop

searching. She had been her protector since childhood, stepping into their mother's role when illness made her too weak to care for them. Darcy had always been the strong one—the determined one—but also the dreamer, forever guiding them towards a better, brighter life.

Darcy's heart broke into a million pieces at the sight of Faith — from the torture and abuse she must have endured, to the sheer strength it must have taken to bring a child into this world alone and terrified. Faith could see the sorrow etched across Darcy's face and clung to her tighter, before breaking down completely, sobbing against her sister's neck. They remained like that for a long while, their tears mingling as years of pain and loss poured out of them both.

Danny quietly approached and lifted the baby from the mattress, holding him gently to offer his own form of comfort and safety. Faith said nothing, her eyes fixed on Darcy with a mixture of love, shock, and disbelief.

Breaking the silence, Darcy asked softly, "Is the baby yours? What's his name?" She didn't want to bring up the past twenty years in that dark, foul-smelling basement — there wasn't time. She needed to get Faith and the baby out, to somewhere safe, to her home — the place that had waited too long for her sister's return.

Faith hesitated. Her voice was frail, her words almost unused from years of isolation. She finally managed to whisper, "Yes, he's my precious boy. I named him Pedar — a mix of you and Penelope." Her smile faltered as she added shakily, "Where's Penelope? Did you find her too? Is she okay?"

Darcy's expression told her everything. Faith's face fell, and she lowered her head, murmuring, "Can we please get out of this hellhole now?"

Danny carefully handed baby Pedar to Darcy before helping Faith to her feet. Faith recoiled at first, uncertain if she could trust him, but relaxed slightly when Darcy gave her a reassuring nod. She allowed him to help her, though her movements were weak and unsteady. Darcy's eyes filled with tears at the sight of what remained of her once lively, radiant sister.

It took time for Faith to climb the steps leading to the dark corridor, the torchlight flickering ahead of them. Darcy cradled Pedar tightly, struggling as he wriggled and whimpered for his mother. She whispered soothingly to calm him as they made their way towards the side exit. Faith leaned on Danny, her strength nearly gone.

When they finally stepped outside, Faith lifted her face to the night sky. The stars shimmered above them, and she inhaled deeply, tears streaming freely down her cheeks. She didn't wipe them away. Instead, she smiled faintly and whispered, almost in awe, "You wouldn't believe how long I've wished for this day — to feel the air, the breeze on my skin, and to see there's still beauty left in this world."

Darcy wanted to refrain from asking but couldn't stop herself. She needed to know. "When was the last time you were outside that building?" she asked quietly.

Faith grimaced, her voice weak but steady. "I believe it may have been five years or more. They took me to a few different rooms within the hospital, but never outside. They wouldn't even let me go to a proper hospital to deliver the baby. I didn't think Pedar would survive — or me, for that matter — but somehow, it's a miracle we're still here. You are the miracle, Darcy, you know that, don't you? I never lost hope that one day you'd rescue me. This is the most precious day of my life — filled with sadness, yes, but also joy. You mean the world to me, Darcy. You always have, and you always will. I know now that I'll always be safe and loved as long as I'm with you."

They embraced again, tears of happiness and relief flowing freely, with little Pedar nestled between them, gurgling contentedly. Darcy asked Danny to fetch the spare clothing from her backpack — items she had packed earlier in the day, just in case. Faith was wearing almost nothing, and what little she had on offered no warmth against the chilly night air, nor comfort for her frail body.

Danny helped Faith dress while Darcy held Pedar close, clutching him protectively as if to shield him from every harm the world could offer. When Faith was finally clothed, Darcy hesitated, then asked softly, "Did any harm come to Pedar?" Her voice trembled — she needed to hear it, to be sure his soul remained untouched.

Faith met her gaze and shook her head. "No," she whispered, eyes glistening with gratitude. Darcy exhaled shakily, relief washing through her. The thought of what could have happened made her sick, but now it was over. At least Faith and her son were safe — the healing could begin.

Danny guided Faith gently into the back of the vehicle while Darcy placed Pedar into her arms, wrapping them both in a thick blanket from the car's boot. Danny then radioed the rest of the group, informing them that Faith had been found alive, and to regroup outside.

One by one, the team emerged from the building, dishevelled and exhausted, looking as though they had been through a boxing match. But their faces brightened at the sight of Faith and her baby. Relief and joy rippled through the group.

As they began securing the premises, one of the members reported to Danny and Darcy that the remaining missing children had been found — hidden away in a concealed closet discovered at the last minute. The team immediately contacted the relevant agencies and authorities to take over, ensuring everyone would finally be safe.

Danny drove Faith and Pedar to the nearest hospital for a full check-up, then took Darcy to the all-night pharmacy where she picked up essential items for both Faith and the baby. Afterwards, Darcy returned to the hospital and stayed with them overnight while they received treatment. Danny went back to the warehouse, promising to return the following day to collect them.

Before he left, Darcy thanked him sincerely for

everything he had done and reached up to kiss him on the cheek. She wrapped her arms around his back, holding on for as long as she could. A pang of regret struck her — she had never experienced this kind of love or compassion from anyone before. Even in the short time she had known this remarkable man, she felt something powerful and real. Darcy knew she wasn't going to let that slip away, and she hoped the feeling wasn't one-sided.

She watched as Danny's car disappeared down the road, then turned and walked back into the hospital. Hunger gnawed at her, so she bought a few snacks from the vending machine before curling up in the chair beside Faith's bed. She sat quietly, watching Faith and Pedar sleeping peacefully. It was, without question, the first real night's sleep Faith had had since before she was taken.

Darcy's thoughts drifted. She wondered how her sister would cope with everything she'd been through — whether she would ever find joy and love for life again. But she reminded herself of Faith's strength, her resilience. The fact that she was still alive was proof enough. Deep down, Darcy knew her sister would heal in time and finally live the life she'd always deserved.

As the nurse tiptoed in to administer more IV vitamins, Darcy's eyes closed. A warm, comforting feeling spread through her body. For the first time in years, she felt peace. They were safe now — and at last, her world felt complete.

Chapter 19

The following three months were a whirlwind of events —
filled with turmoil, triumph, and healing — yet through it all,
Faith and Darcy laughed and loved deeply. Their small
family unit grew stronger by the day, and their health
improved remarkably. Faith had gained weight and was
slowly beginning to feel like her old self again. Months of
therapy and emotional recovery had helped her find peace,
and though she still had a long road ahead, she finally felt
safe after years of torment and abuse.

She now lived with the comforting certainty that she
and Pedar were on their way to a healthy, happy life
alongside Darcy. Surrounded by the extended family of their
group, Merkaba, Faith was constantly overwhelmed by the
love and kindness they showed her. Each week, she and
Darcy met up with their new friends at one another's homes,
sharing home-cooked meals and heartfelt laughter.

Faith's friendship with Rio had blossomed into
something tender and promising — perhaps the beginning of
a long and beautiful relationship. Darcy, meanwhile, was
happily in love with Danny, and an engagement was just

around the corner. Faith had never seen her sister radiate so much warmth and affection for anyone before her abduction, and she doubted she ever would again. The love between Darcy and Danny gave Faith hope that she and Rio might one day share something just as profound.

Both sisters were now proud members of Merkaba and felt honoured to belong to a community that fought for justice every day. They had already helped rescue countless others and vowed to continue doing so for as long as they could — knowing in their hearts that this was part of their soul's purpose.

Not long after the mission, Darcy and Faith brought Penelope home and laid her to rest in the garden, surrounded by her favourite flowers, with ornamental butterflies and dragonflies dancing above her grave. Each week, Darcy placed a single yellow balloon beside the headstone, letting it float freely into the sky — just like Penelope.

It brought comfort to Darcy and Faith to know that all the men captured during the mission were now in prison, and that the main ringleader had been found and brought to justice — not only for the countless lives he had destroyed, but for the life so cruelly taken from them: their beloved

Penelope. Records uncovered at several sites also led to the discovery of the clients involved, and they too were held accountable in court.

Faith later told Darcy that Penelope had been kept in the same locations as her over the years, but had been moved to a different site around six months before Faith was rescued. She had never known where Penelope was taken. The sisters were kept apart throughout their captivity, only catching fleeting glimpses of each other when being transferred between buildings or rooms.

Now, as they all sat around Penelope's resting place in the garden — Danny on Darcy's left, her best friend Marilyn on her right, and Faith and Rio sitting opposite — Darcy found herself reflecting on everything that had led to that moment. She thought of the painful search, the heartbreak, and finally the discovery of Penelope in that makeshift grave all those long, difficult months ago.

Darcy often pondered how she had received Penelope's messages and the instructions that had guided her to the truth. For so long, her heart had insisted there could only be one explanation: that the angels worked in mysterious ways. The signs and synchronicities she witnessed daily felt like constant reminders that she was being guided, that she was on the right path. She truly believed she was supported, protected, and inspired to live each day with love, honour, and light.

Looking around at her wonderful family and friends, Darcy caught her breath. Gratitude flooded her heart as she realised how blessed she was to have all these cherished souls gathered together, laughing, talking, sharing life. And yet, beneath that warmth lay a dawning truth: her journey might not be over. Penelope's story might not be over.

Life, she realised, is truly worth living when you finally understand the life you are meant to live and sometimes, when you are brave enough to follow the signs toward what you're meant to discover next.

Darcy cherished these rare, quiet moments in the garden with Penelope, a precious bubble of peace away from the chaos. She would sit there, lost in thought, replaying memories she held close to her heart. But today, an unshakable unease crept under her skin—a creeping sensation she couldn't quite place. The air suddenly felt heavy, thick with something unsaid, and goosebumps prickled her arms like a warning. It was as if her mind was screaming that something vital was missing, something she'd overlooked.

She tried to brush it off, blaming it on the lingering grief that never truly left her. But no matter how hard she tried, the nagging feeling burrowed deeper, refusing to be ignored. Something was very wrong.

Her thoughts shattered with the sharp, unexpected ring of the doorbell, echoing loudly enough for her to hear even from the garden. She rose, leaving behind the distant shrieks and giggles of Danny and Faith, and made her way through the house to the front door. Pulling it open, she was taken aback to find Detective Karne standing there—the same officer involved in the operation that had rescued Faith all those months ago. That case had been closed. Why was he here now?

Karne shifted awkwardly, twisting his wedding ring round and round, his eyes darting away before settling back on Darcy with a look heavy with worry. "Can I help you, Detective Karne?" she asked, suspicion tightening her chest.

He straightened his tie and buttoned his jacket, clearing his throat as if gathering every ounce of courage. "Sorry to call unannounced, but this can't wait. I didn't want to say this over the phone." He paused, hands stuffed into his pockets, gaze dropping to the floor before meeting hers again. "We've been reviewing the autopsy report from when the coroner first examined Penelope's body. The report went missing in the system for months, only to be found recently buried under a pile of paperwork that was never filed. You were told the cause of death at the time, but there's a crucial detail you were never informed of..." He faltered briefly. "The DNA samples—both yours and Faith's—that were given for comparison don't match the DNA from the body examined at the autopsy. The dental records don't match either."

Darcy's heart pounded. "What are you saying?"

Karne's voice dropped, heavy with the weight of the truth. "The body buried in your garden is not Penelope's. It matches a woman named Rebecca Hick, who vanished nine years ago. Penelope... she may still be alive."

About the Author

Anabel obtained a social work degree and has worked in social care for 20 years. She was born and brought up in Wales, and continues to live in the UK with her two children.

Author Note

I found after writing this book that it has reignited the passion for writing fictional stories from my younger days when I was in school. I have always loved reading a variety of novels, mostly written by my favourite authors, and I often wondered throughout the years of writing my own story one day.

I wanted to bring an emotional journey throughout but also an inspiring story that may resonate with the reader.

Although the story is fictional, my own personal journey of healing and personal growth with my intuition, has also played an important part in the shaping of the story, as well as the signs I encounter regularly.

The story, I feel, also reflects real world events that occur daily, hoping to show more awareness of the realities in everyday life.

Published in Collaboration with Noble Legacy Publishing

www.noblelegacypublishing.co.uk